"GREMLINS REALLY EXIST, YOU'VE JUST GOT TO KEEP WATCHING FOR THEM."

Billy couldn't suppress a smile.

"It's true," said Mr. Futterman. "You think I'm pulling your leg? Gremlins were everywhere during World War Two. We used to see them dancing on the wings of our plane. They played every prank in the book. Once they snuck up to our pilot and shouted, 'You're flying upside down, you fool!' That was really a close one because the pilot turned us over in a split second."

Billy laughed. "You actually saw them?"

"You'd see them out of the corner of your eye, but just as you shot them a full glance, they'd vanish. . . ."

GREMLINS

STARRING ZACH GALLIGAN
PHOEBE CATES·HOYT AXTON·POLLY HOLLIDAY·FRANCES LEE McCAIN
MUSIC BY JERRY GOLDSMITH·EXECUTIVE PRODUCERS STEVEN SPIELBERG
FRANK MARSHALL·KATHLEEN KENNEDY·WRITTEN BY CHRIS COLUMBUS
PRODUCED BY MICHAEL FINNELL·DIRECTED BY JOE DANTE

George Gipe
Based on a Screenplay Written by
Chris Columbus

 CORGI   AVON

A CORGI/AVON BOOK 0 552 52263 5

First publication in Great Britain
Published by arrangement with Avon Books,
959 Eighth Avenue,
New York 10019

PRINTING HISTORY
Corgi/Avon edition published 1984

Made and printed in Great Britain by the
Guernsey Press Co. Ltd., Guernsey, Channel Islands.

Special thanks to the people who helped make my job
Gremlin-free:

Elaine Markson

Kathryn Vought

Dan Romanelli

Mike Finnell

Joe Dante

Brad Globe

Geoffrey Brandt

Judy Gitenstein

Ed Sedarbaum

GREMLINS

PROLOGUE

Many hundreds of years ago on the planet Enz, a great inventor named Mogturmen created a new species of animal. These peaceful and intelligent creatures, which he called Mogwai, were designed to be goodwill ambassadors throughout the universe. Mogturmen wanted them to be living proof that animals and people did not have to kill each other to survive.

Among the first planets selected for Mogwai population were Kelm-6 in the Poraisti Range, Clinpf-A of the Beehive Pollux, and the third satellite of Minor Sun #67672, a small planet known by its inhabitants as Earth.

The people of Enz were pleased, thinking they had done a wonderful thing for the universe.

But then something went wrong. Very wrong.

Soon after the first Mogwai were sent out, it was discovered that Mogturmen's creatures were unstable. Under certain conditions, some changed from gentle beings into monsters. Word came back to Enz describing how the Mogwai started landslides, played tricks on neighboring tribes so that wars broke out, and caused machinery to break down. As a result, no more Mogwai were sent to other planets.

Of the Mogwai who remained on the three colonized planets, most died quickly. When they became terrifying creatures, changes took place inside their bodies that shortened their life spans. Instead of long and peaceful lives, they lived short, exciting ones.

By the early 1980s, there was only one Mogwai left on Earth.

CHAPTER ONE

In a dark corner of the back room of the curio shop, the Mogwai dozed quietly in his cage. The Chinese man who owned him and ran the shop kept him hidden because his customers asked too many questions when they saw the unusual animal.

The Mogwai didn't mind being alone. He had seen how dangerous it was for his species to mix with soci-

ety. It wasn't such a bad life, tucked away in the curio shop. He was happy and comfortable and his
owner fed him regularly. He also was allowed to
wander around the back room among the musty
books, colorful Oriental masks, and ancient Chinese
armor. Looking at all the interesting objects, the
Mogwai felt he could spend a hundred years here
without getting bored.

It was a wonderful place to sleep, too—quiet, cool,
and best of all, dark.

The Mogwai did not like the light.

He was curled into a ball, dreaming, when the Chinese man entered. Holding a small plate in his frail
fingers, the man walked quietly to the cage, lifted
the burlap that covered it, and looked down at his
furry pet. On the plate was an assortment of delica-
cies left over from Han Wu's restaurant next door—
part of an egg roll, some rice, broccoli, and pork
scraps. To these the Chinese man had added a small
piece of cardboard.

He hadn't tossed in the cardboard to be mean. It
was just that he was constantly amazed at the Mogwai's ability to swallow just about anything. The day
before, he had actually eaten a sponge. The day before that, he had eaten some white packing chips.

This wonderful animal must have a stomach like a
garbage disposal, the old man thought, and he wondered how long it would take him to eat the cardboard.

Suddenly aware of his master's presence, the Mogwai stirred, opened his eyes, and bounced up happily
as the food's aroma reached him.

"You may enjoy yourself now, my friend," the
man said softly, patting the Mogwai gently on the
head.

Sniffing at the plate, the Mogwai saw the cardboard and knew immediately from its shape and texture that it was not real food. He knew it probably wouldn't taste very good. He also realized it wouldn't hurt him if he ate it. And the Chinese man so enjoyed seeing him eat unusual objects that the Mogwai decided to humor him once again. He snapped up the cardboard and began to grind it between his teeth. It tasted awful, but the smile crinkling his master's features made eating it almost worthwhile. As he swallowed the last pulpy fragment and began to attack the rice and egg roll, the Mogwai was glad he had made the sacrifice.

It was, he concluded, a small enough price to pay for the peaceful life he led.

* * *

For a moment Billy Peltzer resisted the urge to kick his car. Then he lashed out, driving his boot solidly against the rusting spot where the rear fender met the car's body.

He was immediately sorry. A jolt of pain in his toe caused him to yell angrily. Why did something like this always happen when he was late for work?

He sighed, looked at his watch, and groaned. If he could be shot out of a cannon directly into the bank where he worked, he would be only a minute late. He glanced down the street, hoping to see someone he knew who would give him a lift. There wasn't a car in sight. Kingston Falls, as usual, was nearly deserted.

Even worse, the small town was covered with a thick layer of new snow, which made walking difficult. Getting to work on foot would be like setting out for the North Pole.

Nothing seemed to go smoothly for Billy these

days. He was just a couple of years out of high school and he still wasn't sure what he wanted to do with his life. His mother called it a "difficult" time. Billy knew only that he was mostly restless and bored. Aside from his car breaking down all the time, nothing exciting seemed to happen to him. Working at the bank was not exactly fascinating, but at least it provided him with some spending money for records, clothes, gas for his car (when it worked), and art supplies. He hoped to be able to get his own apartment soon. It wasn't that he disliked living with his parents, but it somehow made him seem juvenile, and he wanted to be independent.

"Broke down again?"

Billy turned to see Murray Futterman, the talkative neighbor around the corner, seated behind the wheel of his snowplow. Even though Billy desperately needed a ride, he hesitated. He knew that Mr. Futterman would talk his ear off the whole time.

. In fact, he had started already. "That doesn't happen with American machinery. Ours can stand up to anything, but an old Volkswagen like that is no good and probably never was. What's the trouble?"

"I'm not sure," Billy replied glumly. "Sometimes it works fine, even in freezing weather. Other times it won't start, even when it's nice."

"Sounds like gremlins to me."

"Gremlins?" Billy repeated.

"Yup, gremlins. Little imps," Futterman said. "They love to fool around with machinery. I saw a lot of 'em during World War Two. I was a tail gunner on a Flying Fortress. Those gremlins used to knock my sights out of line so I'd miss, or they'd chisel tiny holes in the glass windows so that cold air would get in. They'd even slide down the gun barrel and jam the trigger as I was about to fire."

"You're not pulling my leg, Mr. Futterman, are you?" Billy asked with a smile.

"No siree. They were really there. We saw 'em. But you'd better hop on my plow or you'll be late. No other cars in sight."

Billy climbed up beside Mr. Futterman and the plow started off. They had only gone one block, though, when Billy groaned. His golden retriever, Barney, was following them, his big eyes happy, his nose high as it pulled in exciting and unfamiliar smells.

"Want me to turn around and take him back?" Futterman asked.

"No, that's all right," Billy said. "I'll tie him under the counter at the bank. Mr. Corben won't like it, but if Barney's quiet, maybe we can get away with it until lunchtime."

They were only two blocks from the bank when a sudden explosion, accompanied by an arc of red fire, caused the engine to sputter and then die.

"Darn," Futterman rasped. "That happens every once in a while. Wait a minute. I'll have it fixed in a jiffy."

"That's all right," Billy said as he slid to the ground and started the final jog to the bank. As he did, a beeping horn and the crunch of chains against snow brought him to a quick halt.

"Get outa the way, you dumb cat!"

From the window of the Kingston Falls police cruiser, Deputy Brent was shouting at a small furry cat, which stood an inch from the car's front wheels.

"Move, you stupid rat with legs!" Brent shouted.

Billy recognized the cat as one of Mrs. Deagle's. He

ran to the side of the car, scooped the animal into his arms, and trotted back to the curb.

"It's all right," he yelled over his shoulder. "I'll take her back."

A minute later, Billy crossed Mrs. Deagle's lawn and rang her bell. He was rewarded with the sight of her scowling face and her lopsided wig.

"I told you not to walk on the grass," she said sharply.

"I didn't walk on the grass," Billy replied. "I walked on the snow."

"Don't be so smart," Mrs. Deagle shot back.

"Well, I brought back your cat," Billy said. "She was nearly run over by the police car."

"The way you're carrying her, it's lucky she can still walk," the old woman hissed. "Now get your dog off my porch."

Billy turned and left, with Barney close at his heels. At the bottom of the steps, they turned the corner sharply. Barney brushed against the ceramic snowman Mrs. Deagle kept in the yard. The snowman's head plunked into the snow.

"Those destructive little beasts," Mrs. Deagle shouted from the dining room window. "I'll get both of them for that."

* * *

Billy arrived at the bank just a few minutes before customers were to be admitted. He tied Barney below the counter by his chair. Kate, as pretty as ever, smiled shyly at him, and once again Billy resolved to ask her for a date. He had little time to think about it, however, because he was immediately summoned into Mr. Corben's office by Gerald Hopkins, the junior vice-president.

Hopkins, although only twenty-three, was rapidly

approaching middle age. His main ambition in life was to be president of the bank, or at least to reach some position that would allow him to boss people around. He was about to practice on Billy.

Seated behind his mammoth desk, Mr. Corben looked like a judge in his chamber. "Seventeen minutes and thirty-three seconds," he said, glancing at his watch. "That's how late you are. 'Punctuality is the politeness of kings.' Do you know who said that?"

Billy shook his head.

"King Louis the Eighteenth," Corben said. "He was always on time."

"He didn't have an old Volkswagen, I guess," Billy said with a smile.

"If your car's old, get a new one," Gerald snapped. "And don't wear brown shoes with dark blue trousers."

Billy looked at the floor, choked back the angry words he felt, and left.

His troubles had only just begun. Mrs. Deagle was waiting at his counter, cradling the ceramic snowman's head in her arms.

"You and your dog broke this," she said.

"I'm sorry, Mrs. Deagle. How much do I owe you?"

"I don't want money," she shot back. "I want your dog."

"You want Barney? What for?"

"I want to punish him. I want to say, 'Here, Barney. Come here, Barney'—so I can strangle him!"

Barney, hearing his name, rose from his sleeping position beneath Billy's counter, slipped his head free of the leash, and in an instant bounded onto Billy's lap. From there, he hurled himself across the counter onto Mrs. Deagle's shoulders. Beginning with the woman's chin, he proceeded to give her face a thorough licking, causing her to shriek. The ceramic head fell to the floor, shattering into a thousand pieces.

"Help! Help!" Mrs. Deagle screamed as she and Barney toppled to the floor in a tangle of arms, legs, and wet paws.

Instantly the twin figures of Mr. Corben and Gerald Hopkins appeared to assist Mrs. Deagle.

"If I ever see that dog in the bank again, you're fired!" Mr. Corben said.

Back on her feet, Mrs. Deagle shot a hateful glare at Billy. "I'm going to get you and your dog," she threatened. "You just wait."

* * *

Billy's father always had problems getting something different and exciting for his son at Christmas time, and this year was no exception.

Mr. Peltzer had been hoping to find something before heading home from his business trip, but time was getting short. Now, after spending the better part of an afternoon searching for something unique, he found himself in a cellar curio shop in Chinatown. He had been lured there by a Chinese boy of perhaps nine who had overheard him asking for something "different" in another shop.

"What does you son like to do?" the old Chinese man behind the counter asked.

"Well, he's an artist," Mr. Peltzer replied. "A cartoonist. Maybe there's some sort of gizmo in here an artist could use."

"Gizmo?"

"Yeah. A gadget. Like this."

With that, Mr. Peltzer opened his briefcase and brought forth his patented Bathroom Buddy.

"Maybe you could sell a few of these here," he offered. "I invented it myself. It's a combination shaver, toothbrush, and comb. Look, here's where the toothpaste comes out."

He pressed a switch on the side of the device. Immediately a spray of watery white liquid shot out, hit a wall nearby, and dribbled onto the floor.

"No problem," Mr. Peltzer said. "It cleans up easily."

Adjusting the pressure on the device, he attempted to stem the flow of toothpaste but succeeded only in directing a huge glob of white gunk onto his coat.

The old Chinese man and the boy began to laugh uproariously. As they laughed, Mr. Peltzer became aware of a third voice. It was an unearthly laugh, something between the gurgle of an infant and the shriek of a parrot.

"What's that?" Mr. Peltzer called out.

When the old man and boy finally quieted down, their silence isolated the strange laughter. Mr. Peltzer walked toward the back room, which was the source of the sound. "Is that the reason you brought me here?" he asked the boy.

The boy looked at the floor.

"Is it all right to go back there?"

When the old man shrugged, Mr. Peltzer pushed his way through a set of beaded curtains into the back room. On a table in the corner was a small cage draped with a piece of burlap. Lifting the burlap, Mr. Peltzer looked inside at the strange creature.

"What is it?" he asked.

"Mogwai," the Chinese man replied. "It's what he calls himself. I have no idea what it means."

"He's certainly a cute little critter. Tell you what—I'll give you a hundred dollars for him."

"The Mogwai is not for sale."

"Two hundred?"

"No."

"Hey, we'll give him a good home. I promise."

The boy looked quickly at the old man. "Come on, Grandpa," he urged. "Take it. We need the money."

"No. The Mogwai is not like other animals. With Mogwai comes much responsibility. He is not for sale at any price."

With that, the man turned and walked back into the shop.

Mr. Peltzer sighed and slowly pushed the money back into his wallet. "I sure wanted that little gizmo," he said. "You can't reason with him?"

The boy took a deep breath. "My grandfather is right," he said slowly. "The people who have the Mogwai must be very careful. If you owned him, you'd have to keep him out of light, especially bright light. And keep him away from water."

Mr. Peltzer laughed. "I guess that means a day at the beach would be out, huh?"

The boy looked evenly at Mr. Peltzer for a long moment. Finally he spoke.

"O.K., I'll do it. But those are the rules," he said seriously. "If you don't think you can follow them, say so. It's only because we need the money so much that I'll sell you the Mogwai."

"It's a deal," Mr. Peltzer said, handing him the money.

The boy pocketed the money. He took a carved wooden box from the corner table and began to transfer the Mogwai into it. "And I almost forgot the most important thing," he continued. "No matter how much he cries, no matter how much he begs, never *never* feed him after midnight. You got it?"

Mr. Peltzer swallowed back a desire to laugh and nodded. The boy handed him the box and pointed him toward a back door.

"Come on, Gizmo," Mr. Peltzer said softly. "You and me and Billy are gonna be very happy."

CHAPTER TWO

As Billy left the bank late that afternoon, he reflected sadly on the day's events. It was less than a week until Christmas, but he felt less than joyful. His car had refused to start, he had nearly been fired, and Mrs. Deagle had threatened to inflict some terrible vengeance on his dog.

Crossing to the town square, he enjoyed the fresh

pine smell of the Christmas trees for sale there, but continued to think about his own bleak situation. Thus preoccupied, he was a perfect target for a practical joke.

Dressed as a Christmas tree complete with blinking lights and ornaments, thirteen-year-old Pete Fountaine stood perfectly still until Billy was only inches away. He then reached out and grabbed Billy's arm, causing him to jump.

"Got you!" Pete yelled.

Billy smiled. "Yeah. Guess I was daydreaming."

Pete's father, who sold the trees and paid Pete to dress up in the strange outfit, signaled that a customer needed help. Billy and Pete assisted an elderly gentleman as he put the tree into his car trunk.

"Thanks," Pete said. Then, noticing that no other customers were around, he fell into step with Billy. "I want to ask you something," he said. "You've got lots of experience with girls, right?"

"Sure," Billy lied.

"Did you ever ask a girl out?"

"Sure."

"Well, how did you do it? I mean, what did you say?"

Billy shrugged and tried to sound sophisticated. "It depends on the situation," he said. "You've got to be confident, make the girl think you're not scared. And don't let on how much you really like her."

"I get it," Pete said. "Maybe I should zap her with a few insults first, huh?"

"That may be carrying it a bit too far." Billy laughed. "You got anybody in mind?"

"I'll tell you later," Pete said, noticing that his father was looking their way.

Pete went back to work feeling good. It was nice to

know an older person who didn't treat you like a child.

Billy, meanwhile, walked home, thinking of Kate and his cantankerous Volkswagen.

Mrs. Peltzer was in the kitchen. From the expression on her face, Billy knew all was not well.

"I got a call from Mrs. Deagle this afternoon," she began.

"Oh," was all Billy said.

"I know she's an unpleasant person," Mrs. Peltzer said. "But I think you go out of your way to irritate her."

"No, I don't, Mom," he replied. "She's just mean."

"She says you broke her snowman."

"Barney must have bumped it. Did she also tell you I saved one of her cats from being run over?"

"No."

"You see?" Billy muttered. "She only tells you the bad stuff."

The sound of the front door slamming interrupted their conversation. Mr. Peltzer was home from his trip. Caught up in the Christmas spirit, he was out in the hallway singing "Silent Night," his arms loaded with gifts.

Billy and his mother came out of the kitchen to greet him. Their eyes widened at the sight of the presents.

"You can't open any of these yet," Mr. Peltzer said, setting them on the hall table. "Except this one. It can't wait."

Billy took the package from his father and tore away the gift wrap. It was a carved wooden box. He started to lift the cover from the box, but suddenly Mr. Peltzer remembered that the bright hall light violated one of the rules told to him by the Chinese boy. "Let's go into the living room," he said. "It's too bright in here."

"What's inside, a pet bat?" Billy asked.

They went into the living room, where the lighting was more subdued. Billy opened the box and peered inside. "Wow! Look at that thing. What is it?"

"It's called a Mogwai," Mr. Peltzer said proudly.

Kneeling next to the box, Billy studied the creature closely. It was brown and white, about eight inches tall, with long pointed ears and huge brown expressive eyes. It stood upright like a human being, and its body was covered with soft fluffy fur except for the ears. He had a ring of white fur around one eye. A cute pug nose added a special sweet touch to the animal.

"He's cute, all right," Mrs. Peltzer said. "Did he come with any papers? Does he need shots? Is he housebroken?"

"I guess we'll find out soon enough," Mr. Peltzer said. "I didn't have time to check all that out."

"He's a great little guy," Billy said.

"His name is Gizmo."

Billy lifted the creature, cuddling him to his chest. Mrs. Peltzer couldn't resist the temptation to capture the moment on film. Grabbing up her Instamatic camera, she quickly framed the shot and pushed the button.

Gizmo let out a loud shriek, threw himself over Billy's shoulder, and darted beneath the sofa.

"What happened?" Billy cried.

"I forgot to tell you," Mr. Peltzer explained. "The little fella's afraid of light. The flashbulb must have really scared him."

As Billy tried to coax Gizmo out from beneath the sofa, his father told them about the other rules concerning water and feeding the animal after midnight.

"That's the craziest thing I've ever heard," Mrs. Peltzer said. "What difference does it make when he eats?"

Billy shrugged. "Well, my room is perfect for him," he said. "It's pretty dark on the top floor, there's no water, and there's no way he can get food unless I give it to him."

"Good," Mr. Peltzer said, delighted that his son seemed to enjoy the present he had gone to so much trouble to find.

* * *

A short time later, safe and warm in his new home, Gizmo was sleeping comfortably in his box under Billy's drawing table.

Billy was busy working on a sketch. As he drew, the lines on the paper became recognizable forms. One was a muscular warrior battling a horrifying giant with a face that closely resembled Mrs. Deagle's. The warrior was defending a beautiful young woman who was a look-alike for Kate.

Billy was so absorbed in the drawing that he didn't hear the doorbell ring. His mother had to call up the stairs twice before she got his attention.

"It's Pete!"

Because he had no friends his own age with that name, Billy asked: "Pete who?"

"Pete the Christmas tree," Pete Fountaine called from the steps.

"Come on up and see Gizmo," Billy said.

"Who's Gizmo?" Pete asked as he entered the room.

"He's my new pet."

"Your father and I are going out for dinner," Mrs.

Peltzer called. "There's some ice cream in the freezer if you want a snack."

"Thanks, Mom."

Pete stopped short and looked around the room with wide eyes. The walls were covered with drawings of space monsters and warriors, as well as Billy's own sketches. "Boy, this is great," he said. "You got a lot of room here. I have to share with my crummy brother."

At that moment Pete caught sight of the box. He walked over to it and looked inside at Gizmo.

"Holy cow," he said. "What kind of animal is that?"

"I don't know," Billy replied as he lifted him onto the drawing table.

Pete's eyes lit up. "Suppose it's a new animal?" he said. "One of a kind? One that's never been discovered before?"

"Well, suppose it is," Billy said.

"Mr. Hanson was telling us about that," Pete said.

"Mr. Hanson the biology teacher?" Billy asked, remembering the name from school.

"Yeah. He said people discover new animals all the time, and when they do, they get rich and famous."

"That's interesting," Billy said. "But if that would mean I'd have to sell Gizmo, I wouldn't do it."

"You could take pictures and sell them," Pete offered.

The telephone rang. It was Kate, much to Billy's surprise. His expression immediately brightened.

"I thought maybe you could help me with something," Kate began.

"Sure. Anything. What?"

"I'm trying to get signatures on a petition, and I

thought we could go to some people's houses after I get off work at Dorry's."

"Sure," Billy agreed. "What's the petition for?"

"It's against," Kate said. "Against Mrs. Deagle."

Billy laughed. "I'll sign that myself. Where are we going to send her now that Devil's Island is closed?"

Kate laughed. "I found out she's planning to fore-close a lot of mortgages so she can sell a big hunk of property to Hitox Chemical Corporation. That would mean that a lot of people in Kingston Falls would lose their homes and businesses."

"Is that illegal?" Billy asked.

"No, but one of the properties is Dorry's Pub, which is practically a national landmark. Anyway, I figure if we can get enough signatures to stall her awhile, maybe the deal will fall through."

"Count me in," Billy said.

"Can you pick me up between nine-thirty and ten?" she asked. "That's when I get off work."

"Sure," Billy said. "I'll be there."

He was so caught up in the conversation that he failed to see Gizmo wander across the table. He was in the process of hanging up when he saw everything happen at once—Pete reaching for Gizmo . . . the sleeve of Pete's jacket catching on the edge of a can Billy used for soaking brushes . . . the can tipping . . . a splash of water falling to the floor . . . then an-other splash of water falling onto Gizmo's back.

"No!" Billy shouted.

But it was too late. Gizmo's high-pitched scream told him the damage had already been done. The creature's eyes grew wide, his body began to shake, and he rolled across the drawing board. A crackling sound, like a forest fire, seemed to come from his body.

"What did I do?" Pete asked, panicked.

"It's the water," Billy said. "It's not your fault."

Gizmo looked as if he were about to burst. Five huge spots had formed on his back where the water had landed. Now they were growing like blisters. From one of the blisters, a small furry ball suddenly popped out.

Pete and Billy retreated, horrified and fascinated at the same time.

A second ball popped loose from another blister, followed by a third, a fourth, and a fifth. Then, almost as quickly as it had started, it was over. Gizmo's breathing returned to normal and the five patches on his back began to disappear.

If it weren't for the five furry balls on the drawing table, Billy and Pete might have thought they had imagined the whole thing.

"Thank goodness," Billy breathed. "I think he's all right."

"But what are those things?" Pete asked.

The five furry balls had already started to grow and form themselves into shapes similar to Gizmo. Soon it was obvious that more tiny Mogwai had been created. The two boys watched, astounded, as the new creatures grew before their very eyes.

"This is better than 'Twilight Zone,'" Pete murmured.

"I just wonder what my folks are gonna say," Billy muttered.

Now the five new Mogwai were half as large as Gizmo.

"Can I have one?" Pete asked.

Billy shook his head. "Not until we find out what they are. They may be dangerous or something."

"Maybe tomorrow we should take one to the biology lab and find out," Pete offered.

"That's a good idea," Billy replied.

By the time Pete left an hour later, the new Mogwai were fully grown.

Billy found a large cardboard box and put the new Mogwai inside. He noticed that one of the newcomers was slightly larger than the rest. He had a thick mane of white fur down his back.

"I'll call you Stripe," Billy said, petting him.

The Mogwai looked back at him with a stare of evil intensity.

Suddenly Billy knew that even though the new arrivals looked like Gizmo, they were not the same.

He fed them some chicken from the refrigerator and then lay across his bed, trying to make sense out of the strange events of the evening.

* * *

How long Billy slept he couldn't say. He awoke with a start and the feeling that something was wrong.

The room was dark. Completely dark. Even the small desk lamp, which had been on when he fell asleep, was now off.

Had his parents come home and turned off the light? It seemed unlikely they would do such a thing, leaving him lying there in his clothes. Maybe there had been a power failure.

He lay still for a long while. In the background he could hear a rustling sound, low voices—the sort of noise you hear at a surprise party when everyone is trying to be quiet. It was eerie.

Taking a deep breath, Billy swung himself off the bed. A split second later, he found himself lying facedown on the floor.

His legs were paralyzed!

A chorus of hysterical giggles filled the room and continued for nearly a minute.

"What's going on here?" Billy hissed.

He dragged himself in the direction of his desk, found the lamp switch, and turned it on. The small light went on and he sighed with relief.

He looked down at his legs.

They were taped together.

He could hardly believe his eyes, but the evidence was clear. Three neat bands of silver tape encircled his legs—one at the ankles, another just below the knees, and a third just above the knees. No one could have done it but the new Mogwai.

Billy ripped off the tape, turned on another light, and looked around. The Mogwai, except for Gizmo, were gone.

They must have watched him, enjoying their practical joke, until he tore away the tape. Billy could hear their giggles fading as they bounced down the hall steps.

He followed. The going was difficult, though. Like a retreating army burning bridges behind them, the Mogwai had turned off every light as they passed it. Muttering to himself, Billy turned each one back on, trying to locate the creatures by their telltale sounds.

Halfway down the steps, he slipped on a strange object and rolled to the bottom. All around him were plastic dishes, which had been placed on the stairs.

"I can't believe this," Billy muttered.

After several minutes, he located all five new Mogwai. One was in the living room under the sofa, gleefully shredding the evening paper. A second had turned on the television set in the den, found a jar of mustard, and was busily painting the screen. The one with the white fur was carefully arranging items in the pantry so that they would fall at the slightest touch. The fourth and fifth were playing catch with the laundry.

Fortunately, all of them were so involved in their own mischievous projects that they barely noticed Billy. He was unsure how to capture them until he remembered Barney's travel box. It was a large plywood case with handles and a lid that locked. Billy had purchased it several years before during a brief period when Barney was refusing to go to the vet's without a fight. Billy found the box in the garage and brought it back into the house. Finally he was able to round up the Mogwai one by one. None of them put up much of a struggle except Stripe, who threw handfuls of pancake mix at Billy until Billy grabbed him and threw him in the box.

Taking the box upstairs, Billy made sure it was locked and then returned to clean up the damage the Mogwai had done. Only after he went through the entire house to make sure everything was in order did he glance at the clock.

It was eleven-thirty. He had forgotten all about his date with Kate!

"Well," he murmured. "It looks like my first date with her was probably my last."

With that unhappy thought on his mind, Billy drifted into a troubled sleep.

Billy Peltzer's father (right) shops for a special Christmas gift in an old curio shop.

Mr. Peltzer proudly hands Billy the gift while Mrs. Peltzer looks on.

Billy Peltzer.

Kate Beringer.

Billy, Gizmo, and Billy's friend Pete Fountaine.

The new Mogwai sleep peacefully next to Billy's bed.

Billy and Pete take one of the new Mogwai to Mr. Hanson, the biology teacher.

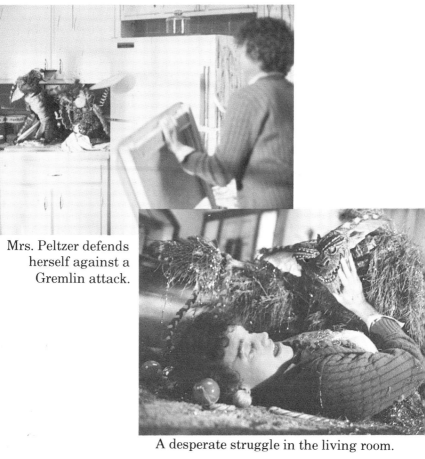

Mrs. Peltzer defends
herself against a
Gremlin attack.

A desperate struggle in the living room.

Billy trails Stripe to the YMCA building.

Before Billy's eyes, the swimming pool rumbles, churns, and roars.

Mrs. Deagle takes her last ride.

With a tremendous growl, the snowplow comes to life and leads straight for Mr. Futterman.

The Gremlins take over Dorry's Pub…

…then the movie theatre.

Billy and Kate escape just in time as…

…the theatre, filled with Gremlins, blows up.

Safe at last!

Billy tracks down Stripe
in the department store.

"Bye, Billy."

CHAPTER THREE

The next morning, Billy told his parents what had happened. He waited for the shock to wear off before he brought up the obvious question. What were they to do with not one, but six Mogwai?

"Well, they are cute," his mother said. "But they sure are mischievous. Keeping all of them is out of the question."

"Why not drop the new ones off at the Humane Society?" Mr. Peltzer suggested.

"If they're a rare species, they may be valuable," Billy replied. "Besides, if they multiply when they're touched with a few drops of water—"

"That's right," his father agreed. "The world could be crawling with those things if people aren't careful."

"Maybe we should just wait until Mr. Hanson examines them," Billy said.

"All right." Mrs. Peltzer nodded. "But if they're going to be here even a couple of days, I don't want them cooped up in that box. It's cruel."

"We can't let them run loose," Billy said. "They might get into the showers or the kitchen or the bathrooms. If they get near water again, we'll have hundreds of them."

"They can stay in your room," Mrs. Peltzer said. "We'll keep the door shut all the time."

With the crisis temporarily over, Billy left for work. He dreaded seeing Kate because he knew she would act cool to him. And he was right. Several times he tried to get her attention, but she just looked away. Even worse, when he tried to explain, she pretended to be busy with something. "She'll never talk to me again," Billy said with a sigh.

The day passed slowly, but finally work was over. Catching up with Kate just outside the bank, Billy grabbed her gently by the arm.

"I'd like to tell you what happened last night," he said.

"It's not necessary," Kate replied. "Maybe I'm a little crazy about Mrs. Deagle's plan to kick people out of their homes. I can't expect everybody to be as gung ho about it as I am."

"But I'm gung ho, too," Billy said. "I really meant to be there last night, except something terrible happened."

"All right," Kate said. "What was it?"

As Billy hesitated, trying to think of a logical way to begin his explanation, Pete Fountaine ran up. "Come on, Billy," he said. "Mr. Hanson's waiting for us. He says he'll look at one of those things now."

Billy looked at Kate. "Have you got a few minutes?" he asked. "Maybe showing you what happened last night will be easier than trying to explain it."

Kate nodded. They all hopped in Billy's Volkswagen, now back among the living, and drove to his house. When they arrived there, Kate was properly impressed at the sight of the Mogwai. "I've never seen anything like this."

"Wait till we get to school," Billy said. "The next part is even more amazing."

Fifteen minutes later, with one of the new Mogwai in a shoe box, Billy, Kate, and Pete arrived at the school. Mr. Hanson, an athletic-looking man in his thirties, looked up and smiled when they entered the biology lab. "Let's see what we have," he said.

Before opening the box, Billy dimmed the lights and pulled down the window shades, an act that amused Mr. Hanson.

But the smile changed to a look of amazement a moment later. "I have no idea what this thing is," he said.

"If it's a new species, we'll be rich," said Pete. "Tell me we'll be rich."

"Where did you get this?" Hanson asked Billy.

"My dad bought it in Chinatown."

"Could I keep it for a few days?"

"Yes, but there are some important rules you'll have to follow." He listed the restrictions on water, bright light, and feeding after midnight.

"All right," Hanson agreed. "But you're sure you're not kidding me?"

Billy shook his head. "If you want a demonstration . . ."

He picked up an eyedropper and loaded it from the sink, then very carefully deposited a single drop of water on the Mogwai's back. For a long moment, nothing happened. Then the crackling sounds started and the creature began to shriek wildly. Kate, her hands over her face, leaped back, then slowly spread her fingers to peer out at the Mogwai's writhings. A minute later, as the frying sounds grew even louder, a huge blister appeared on the Mogwai's skin, broke apart, and sent out a fur ball.

Billy, Kate, Pete, and Mr. Hanson watched as the ball grew and formed itself into a miniature version of its parent.

"That's incredible!" Hanson breathed.

"Well, it looks like we're *all* gonna be rich," Pete said.

Billy looked at Kate and smiled. "I hope you believe me now," he said.

Her expression told him that she did.

* * *

Billy left the newest Mogwai with Mr. Hanson and brought the other one back home. That evening he spent a couple of hours with Kate, collecting signatures for her petition. It was not exactly an exciting date, but he enjoyed being with her. Returning at eleven o'clock, he decided to relax by drawing and watching TV.

As he was settling in, the five new Mogwai stirred

from a long sleep and began to whine for food. Billy tossed them a handful of chocolate candy kisses, which they devoured, foil and all, in a matter of seconds.

The begging sounds promptly started again with renewed urgency.

Billy looked at the electric clock next to the TV. It was eleven-thirty. There was time enough to feed them before midnight, but he was too lazy to move.

"Forget it, fellas," he said. "You had a big meal earlier. Now go to sleep."

To Billy, they didn't seem to like the idea, especially Stripe, who was whining more loudly than the others. After a few more minutes with no response from Billy, Stripe decided to do something desperate.

The young man seemed absorbed in the flickering box on the drawing table. Stripe noticed that a cord ran from the box into the wall, which he concluded was its source of power. If he turned off the box, the young man would realize they were serious and give them food. Slipping away from the other Mogwai, he slithered to the wall and chewed through the cord.

The sound coming from the flickering box did not stop.

Stripe cursed in Mogwai language. What had gone wrong?

What he did not know was that instead of chewing through the cord of the television set, he had caused the electric clock to stop.

Stripe returned to the box, shook his companions awake, and urged them to make another attempt at getting food by making noise. After twenty full minutes of whining and begging, they finally got Billy's attention. Remembering how he felt when he was really hungry, Billy became more sympathetic. Looking at the clock, he saw that it was only eleven-forty. It was still safe to feed them.

"All right," he said. "I'll get you something, but you'll have to eat it quickly."

He raced down to the kitchen, found some left-overs in the refrigerator, and brought them up to the Mogwai. As he rolled up the piece of foil on which he had served them, he noticed that Gizmo had slept through the whole meal.

"Well, I'll make it up to him tomorrow," he said.

He turned off the light and fell into bed.

* * *

Billy awakened after a dreamless night and glanced out the window. It was just beginning to get light. He looked at the clock.

It said eleven-forty.

His mind, which was still not alert, could not understand what it meant. Had he overslept?

Closing his eyes, Billy rolled over and fell back asleep. Then suddenly he sat upright in bed.

The clock still said eleven-forty, but it was now fully light out.

Billy's eyes traveled to the wall outlet, and he saw the chewed ends of the cord. He heard Gizmo making sharp, panicked noises, and at precisely the same moment he saw new shapes in the semidarkness of his room.

There were five of them—huge pods, each larger than a watermelon, with skins that were slimy and soft. A faint crackling noise came from each of the pods. They seemed to bubble slightly, changing shape and texture even as Billy watched them.

The telephone rang. It was Roy Hanson.

"Billy," he said. "Something's happened. I don't

know if there's any connection or not, but I forgot what you said about not feeding the Mogwai after midnight. I left a sandwich near the cage and this morning it was gone. And in the Mogwai's place—"

"—is a monster pod," Billy said. "Like a big blister?"

"Yes," Mr. Hanson nearly shouted. "That happened to your animals too?"

"I fed them by mistake," Billy replied. "The clock wasn't running, and I didn't realize what time it was."

"Maybe this was something that would have happened anyway," Hanson suggested. "Maybe it had nothing to do with food—"

"No," Billy said. "The Mogwai who didn't eat is O.K."

"Oh."

"What are they, anyway?" Billy asked.

"It looks to me like an animal in the pupal stage," Hanson said, "like a caterpillar in its cocoon. The pods will probably break open and a new form will come out."

"Probably a monster."

"Not necessarily. It could be like a butterfly."

"What should we do?"

"Nothing for the moment. I don't think they're dangerous. Give me your number at work and we'll keep in touch."

Billy gave him the number of the bank, hung up, and stepped gingerly out of bed. After getting dressed, he put Gizmo in a knapsack and took him downstairs. Mrs. Peltzer's face registered shock and amazement as Billy told her about the latest disaster.

"Well," she said. "You'd better get to work. I'll keep a close watch on them."

"I don't like leaving you here alone, Mom."

"Don't be silly," she replied. "I promise to run at the first sign of trouble."

Billy was kept so busy at the bank that the bizarre happenings at his own house seemed faraway—like a science-fiction movie. Shortly before closing time, the figure of Gerald Hopkins appeared at his side.

"There's a personal telephone call for you," he said. "Make it quick. You know we don't like employees getting personal calls."

Billy went to the phone. It was Roy Hanson with a simple message.

"It hatched."

"What did it become?" Billy asked.

"Well, it's no butterfly," Hanson said. "I haven't gotten close to it yet. Why don't you stop by after work and have a look?"

"O.K.," Billy said. "I'll call home first, and if everything's all right there, I'll see you soon."

A half hour later, after checking to make sure that his mother was O.K. and flying out of the bank, Billy pulled up in front of the deserted high school. His footsteps echoed through the empty halls as he raced toward Mr. Hanson's lab.

"Mr. Hanson!" he called out.

There was no reply.

The lab was quiet and dark.

Before he could reach for the light switch, Billy saw two things that chilled his blood.

Lying in the corner of the lab was Mr. Hanson. One leg was bent back beneath him and he stared vacantly at the ceiling. It could mean only one thing!

There was blood and a series of sharp gashes on his neck.

The second thing he saw was even more frightening. Less than ten feet away from him, perched on a countertop and ready to spring, was the most hideous-looking monster he had ever seen.

CHAPTER FOUR

Splat.

Stripe's right arm shot like a rocket through the wet mass on the floor of Billy's bedroom and rose high in a salute of triumph.

But what an arm! No longer ending with a soft furry paw, it was now nearly two feet long and it rippled with muscles. His scaly skin was ringed with white, green, and brown stripes. His bony fist ended in three giant claws, each sharpened to a glistening point.

He was no longer a Mogwai, Stripe knew. He was a Gremlin.

Worming free of the pod, he looked down at the rest of his new body. The soft brown Mogwai fur had been replaced by dark green rippled armor plating. Along his back was a ridge of armor, like that of a prehistoric reptile. His mouth was bloodred and huge, with monstrous fangs protruding from his jaws.

Bouncing lightly on the tips of his clawed feet, he savored the realization that now he was truly powerful. Grinning with anticipation, he looked at the other pods.

"Hurry, hurry, hurry," he hissed gleefully at them. "We've got work to do, great and horrible fun to enjoy."

A minute later, his four Gremlin cohorts popped loose of the pods, shook the debris from their heads and shoulders, and started downstairs behind Stripe.

Below them, Mrs. Peltzer heard the commotion. Sensing danger, she walked cautiously out of the kitchen and toward the source of the noise.

At first she saw nothing. A moment later, something shattered against the wall just above her head. Mrs. Peltzer screamed, setting off a series of hysterical giggles.

All of a sudden, the Gremlins were everywhere.

Twisting her head, Mrs. Peltzer saw four of them right away. One stood near the china cabinet in the dining room, hurling dishes. Two were in the kitchen, going through the pots and pans, tossing them backward onto the floor. The fourth was in the pantry, emptying the contents of every carton and jar onto the floor.

Mrs. Peltzer had the urge to run. But strangely, her fear was overpowered by anger. They were destroying *her* kitchen!

She raced back into the kitchen and grabbed the first thing she saw—a sharp knife.

"Get out of my house!" she yelled.

The order set off a new wave of giggles. The Gremlins proceeded to throw everything at *her*. A coffee mug struck her on the head and pancake flour poured down onto her from above.

Furious now, Mrs. Peltzer lashed out at the closest Gremlin, killing it with the knife. Then she swung at a second, which roared and hurled its own barrage of kitchen knives at the woman. Mrs. Peltzer swung again with the knife, causing the Gremlin to stumble backward. In doing so, one of its clawed fists became caught in the top of Mr. Peltzer's orange-juice squeezer on the counter. Mrs. Peltzer rushed forward and hit the ON switch. With a loud whirr, the powerful engine drew the Gremlin's arm deep into the machine. Screaming, the Gremlin began to spin round and round, its arm disappearing up to its shoulder. A greenish mush spewed out of the juice spout. Soon the entire Gremlin was sucked into the machine and turned into pulp.

A second later, a barrage of heavy objects struck Mrs. Peltzer as the other Gremlins counterattacked. Slipping on the wet floor, she fell, and for an instant she could see only the Gremlins ready to pounce. Her hand grasped a cold metal object, and she brought it up to protect herself. It was a can of insect spray. Unleashing a heavy blast, she hit one Gremlin directly in the eyes, causing it to fall backward.

Scrambling to her feet, Mrs. Peltzer used the spray to force the other Gremlin back across the counter. When it was in front of the microwave oven, she rushed forward and pushed it inside. Then, after slamming the door shut, she set the temperature to maximum and turned the oven on.

Soon popping sounds from the oven told her that the Gremlin inside was being turned into an oozy green omelet.

Mrs. Peltzer thought there was only one Gremlin left, but suddenly another one appeared from the living room. They landed on her shoulders at the same time, knocking the can from her hand. Screaming with pain and terror as they tore at her with their giant claws, she fell to the floor, wondering if this was the end.

* * *

In Mr. Hanson's lab, Billy grunted as the dark green, armor-plated monster landed on his chest and knocked him against a metal cabinet. Lashing out with his forearm, he gave the creature a hard shot to its head, but it seemed more surprised than hurt by the blow.

A ripping sound caused Billy to look down as he felt the stab of pain. The Gremlin had torn a section of corduroy and flesh from the young man's thigh.

With his last ounce of energy, Billy was able to knock the Gremlin aside. He reached out for a fire extinguisher hanging against the wall and managed to get it in front of him just as the Gremlin sprang again. As it became a blur rushing through the air toward him, Billy hit the ON switch before being knocked to the floor.

The speed of the Gremlin's leap caused its head to fly solidly into the funnel of the fire extinguisher.

Unable to remove its head, it was force-fed the poisonous fumes for a full minute. It thrashed wildly on the floor a final time before it died.

Billy lay still for a while. Then he suddenly leaped to his feet.

"Mom!" he cried out.

Billy raced out of the lab and into his car. He turned the key. His heart pounded as the engine failed to start. With growing fear, he tried again, and this time it roared to life.

Sighing with relief, Billy sped through the streets of Kingston Falls. As he pulled up to his house, he looked into the window and saw a terrifying sight— the gaily decorated Christmas tree in the living room suddenly pitched sideways and fell completely out of view!

"Holy—" he began, slamming on the brakes and throwing the door open.

Stumbling up the steps, he tore into the house in time to see Stripe and the other Gremlin wrestling with his mother, who was trying desperately to protect herself in the tangle of limbs and broken decorations. He grabbed the ornamental sword that hung on the wall over the fireplace and began to swing at the green demons. Stripe ducked out of the way, but the other took the full force of Billy's swing just above the shoulder. The sharp edge of the sword dug into the armor plating, separating the Gremlin's head, which bounced into the fireplace and burned to a crisp.

Billy took off after Stripe, but he wasn't fast enough. Rolling himself into a ball, Stripe hurled himself at the picture window. The glass shattered noisily as he broke through. He landed on the soft snow outside and scurried off into the night.

Billy and his mother looked at each other's wounds, satisfying themselves they were not serious.

"Is Gizmo all right?" Billy asked.

"Yes," Mrs. Peltzer said. "He's still in the knapsack."

Billy found him and started putting on another sweater.

"Where are you going?" his mother asked.

"Out after that last one," Billy said.

"Never mind that. Let Sheriff Reilly find him."

"There's no time, Mom. If that last one reproduces, this mess will start all over again. I've got to find him now."

Waving goodbye, he slung the knapsack and Gizmo over his shoulder and went out into the snowy night.

Fortunately, Stripe's three-pronged tracks were visible in the fresh snow. Billy hoped he wouldn't walk in the streets or follow someone else's tracks. Then he'd never be able to follow him.

They had walked only a short distance when Billy suddenly stopped and whistled.

"Giz, I just thought of something," he said. "Water makes you fellas reproduce, right? And snow is frozen water. But the snow didn't make Stripe multiply. Otherwise, this whole area would be crawling with those monsters. . . . What are they called, anyway? They look like the things Mr. Futterman told me about—Gremlins, right? Anyway, if frozen water has no effect on Stripe, we don't have to worry as long as he's out in the snow. But we do have to hope and pray he doesn't get near warmer water."

Billy wasn't sure Gizmo could understand his line of reasoning, but he needed someone to talk to.

A few minutes later, they lost Stripe's trail in a mess of tracks made by a group of kids singing Christmas carols. Trotting after them, Billy soon caught up. He asked if they had seen a "little fella" wearing a funny costume. He did not want to alarm them by telling them what Stripe really was.

The response from the carolers was immediate.

"Yeah, we saw him," one teenager said. "He was hanging around near the back of the group. But when we tried to find out his name, he ran away."

"Which way did he go?"

"Over toward the Y."

Billy looked off toward the dark building that was the Kingston Falls YMCA. He sighed. It was a perfect place for Stripe to hide.

Trotting toward the building, they picked up the Gremlin tracks again and followed them until they disappeared—just below a broken window.

"Well, Giz," Billy said. "It looks like we have to go inside."

He boosted himself onto the ledge and slid into the darkened building, where he paused a moment, waiting for his eyes to adjust to the blackness. He had a flashlight, but he didn't want to turn it on and give away their position.

For a long moment, the only sound was Billy's and Gizmo's breathing. Then, from a far corner, he heard a muffled giggling sound that was only too familiar to him.

Groping his way toward the phantom voice, he soon found himself at the wire mesh of the equipment cage. As he touched it, Billy felt a hard object strike his head and bounce away. The sound told him he had just been hit by a basketball.

A triumphant giggle broke the silence and echoed throughout the gym.

Swinging the flashlight upward and turning it on, Billy saw Stripe appear, cursing in Mogwai and shielding his eyes from the light. Stripe pulled his head back, slid down the side of the equipment cage, and dashed into the next room. Crouched in the semidarkness, Billy heard his claws scratching against the hardwood floor of the basketball court.

Suddenly Billy realized where the Gremlin was headed—and he panicked. Leaping to his feet, he began to run, at full speed. With the flashlight beam bouncing up and down ahead of him, he turned the corner onto the court in time to spot Stripe at the far end.

"The overhead lights!" Billy gasped. "If we can turn those on before he—"

He raced to the nearest wall and groped for switches but found none.

"Darn!"

Then he was running as fast as he could toward the door at the farthest corner of the huge room—the door that led to the swimming pool!

He was too late.

Stripe was already standing at the opposite end of the Olympic-size pool, hopping up and down, his nostrils inhaling the mist which rose from the water's surface. Did he know that water made them reproduce? Or was the triumphant grin merely accidental? Billy wasn't sure. He wondered if there was any way he could frighten Stripe or divert his attention so that he would stay away from the water.

"Wait—" he cried out as the Gremlin seemed to lean forward.

As if in slow motion, Stripe slipped into the pool.

As Stripe disappeared beneath the surface, Billy ran to the far end of the pool and shone his flashlight into the water. The Gremlin had sunk gently to the bottom and was lying facedown, his arms relaxed at his sides. For a moment Billy began to hope that nothing would happen.

A gentle rumbling destroyed the hope. Stripe's back was aflame with tiny pods. They popped from his body and spread across the surface of the pool, dividing and redividing, churning the water into a green froth. The gentle rumbling soon became a roar.

Billy and Gizmo watched, horrified, but for only a moment. Then they half ran, half stumbled out of the building.

CHAPTER FIVE

Collapsing on a gentle slope about fifty yards from the YMCA building, Billy and Gizmo looked sadly at the scene below them. First one form, and then dozens, moved past the windows. Each was a fully grown Gremlin! The unearthly sounds they made added to the horror of the scene.

There's no hope now, Billy thought.

As he and Gizmo had scrambled up the hill only minutes before, he had thought there was a possibility of dealing with the Gremlins. His plan had been to call the fire department and have them set the building ablaze. The pods would have been consumed before they had a chance to hatch. But the Gremlins obviously reproduced much faster than the Mogwai.

Now there were hundreds of them. "What can we do, Giz? I guess there's nothing left but to go to the police."

Billy dreaded the very thought. Going to the police would mean telling them a "wild" story they were likely to laugh at. But he could think of no alternative.

A quarter hour later he was at the tiny Kingston Falls police station. He told his story as simply as possible. Sheriff Reilly and Deputy Brent were more amused than angry at Billy's interruption of their peaceful evening.

"So it's Gremlins you're seeing?" Reilly said. "Little monsters?"

"That's right."

"Green, right?" the sheriff continued, winking at Brent. "Little monsters are always green, you know."

"Well," Billy admitted, "they're mostly green, I guess." He wished they were some other color.

"How many green monsters?" Brent asked.

"I couldn't count," Billy replied. "I imagine a couple of hundred, at least."

"Any idea where these Gremlins come from?"

"My father gave me one as an early Christmas present a few days ago."

"Does your father usually give you monsters for presents?" Reilly asked.

"No," Billy replied, looking down at his shoes. He was beginning to feel silly. "You see, they aren't vicious at first. They're like—"

Suddenly remembering Gizmo, he opened the knapsack and let them have a look. "They're like this one at first," he said. "Very cute and gentle. But if you do the wrong thing, they turn into Gremlins."

"And what's 'the wrong thing,' sonny?" Brent asked with a grin.

Billy swallowed and plunged ahead. "Well, if you feed them after midnight—"

Reilly choked on his drink. "Feed them after midnight?" he screamed, dribbling coffee down both sides of his mouth. "I find that hard to believe, son. Are you saying this little thing here turns into a green monster if he eats after midnight?"

"Yes," Billy said.

Reilly wiped his mouth and smiled.

"Suppose he eats at ten o'clock at night and gets something stuck between his teeth," Brent asked, smiling wickedly. "And suppose that something comes loose after midnight. Does that something count as food if he swallows it?"

Without waiting for an answer, Reilly said, "Does a liquid count as food even though he don't have to chew it?"

"Anything with calories," Brent replied.

The two officers continued as if Billy weren't there. Suddenly Billy knew it was hopeless.

"Look, let's forget it," he said. "I just came to tell you there may be calls tonight from people being bothered or attacked by monsters. I hope that doesn't happen, but if it does, you'll know I was tell-ing the truth.''

He closed the knapsack cover on Gizmo and strode out of the police station.

As he walked into the cold night, he heard the po-licemen's voices erupt again in uproarious laughter.

* * *

The series of strange events that was to paralyze Kingston Falls began a few minutes later. It started innocently enough when a traffic light at the inter-section of Randolph Road and Route 46 began show-ing green in all four directions. Cars whizzed through the crossroads, missing each other by inches. Then two cars going one way and a tractor trailer the other crashed in a nasty pileup.

Not far away, another traffic light began showing red in all four directions. Cars were backed up for miles with hundreds of people stuck inside.

Meanwhile, on Delta Drive, pedestrians and mo-torists alike were attacked by hundreds of runaway tires, which somehow had gotten loose from a ware-house nearby. Several cars were dented and one woman was badly cut when she leaped out of the way of a tire into a utility pole.

At the Governor's Mall Shopping Plaza, brooms started falling from the roof and the automatic doors slammed shut on several customers.

Billy, driving home, knew nothing of these inci-dents, but he sensed that bad things were happen-ing. When he saw Father Bartlett outside the church, he decided to warn him. He pulled the car to the curb and rolled down the window.

"Father Bartlett," he cried. "Please go back inside. It's not safe out here."

The priest smiled indulgently. "I'm just going down to the mailbox to send off a few last-minute Christmas cards," he said. "What's the matter?"

"No time to explain now," Billy said. "I just think you and everyone else should stay inside."

"Well, I promise to do that as soon as I've mailed these," Bartlett said.

As Billy drove off, he walked to the corner mailbox, pulled down the door, and dropped his letters inside.

A second later, the letters flew back at him, hit the front of his coat, and fell to the snow.

Blinking, Father Bartlett retrieved the letters, opened the mailbox door, and peered into the blackness. Seeing nothing, he pushed the letters inside.

Again they flew back.

Now he was sure something was wrong. Could it be one of those hidden camera tricks they pull on people and show on TV?

Shrugging, Father Bartlett decided to have one more try at mailing the letters. He pulled down the door and reached inside. His hand was gripped by a cold, sharp object. As he started to pull away, a claw reached out of the mailbox and began to encircle his neck.

"This has gone far enough!" Father Bartlett cried. Twisting and turning, he began to scream for help as his head slowly disappeared into the mailbox.

* * *

"The man on the radio said it must be Gremlins," Mrs. Futterman said to her disgruntled husband.

"Maybe he meant it as a joke," Murray Futterman growled. He was angry because the television set had just broken. There was no way to get a picture on any station, and the only help in sight was some fool on the radio saying it was Gremlins.

He moved quickly toward the hall closet. "I'm going to check the antenna," Futterman snarled. "Maybe it blew over."

Pulling on a jacket, he walked outside to the yard and looked up at the roof. The antenna was still intact but it was surrounded by three small, long-armed figures that brought back memories of World War II.

"By golly!" he said. "It *is* Gremlins."

Remembering his shotgun in the locked closet at the back of the garage, he squeezed past the snow-plow, which was so wide it left only six inches on either side. He got the gun, ran out to the driveway, and aimed at one of the Gremlins.

Bam!

One of the green demons fell off the roof.

Futterman laughed. It felt good to fire the gun again.

A low chattering sound distracted him momentarily, but not for long. He was more interested in getting the other troublemakers. Once again he fired, and a second Gremlin fell.

In his excitement to bag the third Gremlin, Futterman hardly heard the snowplow roar to life. As the last Gremlin on the roof started to hop to safety, Futterman got him in his sights. "Oh, no you don't," he hissed.

Now the snowplow seemed to lean forward. Its engine roared.

Bam!

"Hot darn!" Futterman cried out. "I got you, you little—"

He never completed the sentence. With a tremendous growl, the snowplow tore out of the garage headed straight for Mr. Futterman. . . .

* * *

Mrs. Deagle was seated in her automatic stair-climbing device when the doorbell rang.

"Blast!" she whined. "Who can that be at this hour?"

The stair-climbing device had been recommended by her doctor so that she would not strain her heart. It was basically a wheelchair attached to a motor and pulley, and it enabled Mrs. Deagle to go up and down the stairs without effort.

The doorbell rang again. Mrs. Deagle angrily dismounted and started for the door. Earlier that evening, young people singing Christmas carols had interrupted her dinner and she had sent them away. Was this another group? As the doorbell rang a third time, Mrs. Deagle went into the kitchen and grabbed a broom. This time she would show them her own brand of Christmas spirit!

Flinging the door open, she choked on the angry words she'd prepared for the unwanted callers. The group was the strangest she had ever seen, looking like something left over from Halloween. All of them were very short, singing a mumbo-jumbo tune that was totally incomprehensible.

"Get out of here!" Mrs. Deagle shouted. "I don't

want to hear you or see you! Those costumes are terrible."

As she spoke, two Gremlins slipped unnoticed
through the open door and into the house. Mrs. Deagle, holding the broom, rushed toward the others and
shooed them off the porch.

"And stay away!" she shouted after them.

Going back inside, she walked to the stair-climber
and turned the switch to UP. One of the Gremlins
watched, fascinated. Meanwhile, the second Gremlin began to eat some of the cats' food in the kitchen,
causing an instant uproar from Mrs. Deagle's collec-
tion of cats. The Gremlin ran into the dining room.

"What's that commotion?" Mrs. Deagle cried.

She put the machine in neutral and walked toward the kitchen.

When she turned the corner, the Gremlin in the
hallway began twisting wires in the stair-climber's
control panel. Mrs. Deagle returned to the chair and
sat down.

"At last," she wheezed. "A moment to relax."

As she spoke, she shifted the chair into gear and
pushed the switch back to UP.

The chair hesitated momentarily, then suddenly
lurched up the stairs. Mrs. Deagle gasped and
clutched the arm rests as the seat, gathering speed
at a frightening rate, raced past the pulley, smashed
through the hall window, and carried the screaming
woman into the cold night.

                          * * *

Billy was nearly home when he turned on the car
radio and heard the news reports. There were ac-
counts of people stepping into open manholes, being

attacked by all sorts of flying objects, finding bricks
laid across roads, seeing strange small creatures . . .
and then Mr. Futterman, run over by his snowplow . . . Mrs. Deagle, found in her chair in the field
behind her house . . .

"Good grief," he muttered. "It's worse than I
thought."

Another report caused his hair to nearly stand on
end.

The creatures were reported in Dorry's Pub.
That was where Kate worked!

Billy hit the brakes so quickly his car did an automatic U-turn in the middle of the street. Suppose
Kate was trapped in there! He had to find out if she
was safe.

* * *

Kate was, indeed, quite trapped. A half hour before, about fifty green demons had entered the pub.
The few customers had managed to escape. So had
Dorry himself, but Kate had been behind the bar and
she was trapped inside.

Now she was exhausted and terrified. The pub
looked like a cross between the winner's headquar-
ters on election night and D-day at Omaha Beach.
The floor oozed with spilled drinks, bits of food, and
crushed popcorn. The air was filled with flying
objects—bottles, billiard balls, chairs, whatever
wasn't nailed down. A noisy and confusing babble of
squeals and giggles made Kate's head spin. Gremlins were everywhere.

Her only slim chance for escape lay in the knowl-
edge that Billy's creatures were terrified of bright
lights. If she could only find a way to produce light,

she might get out. The problem was that the bar was dimly lit. There didn't even seem to be a flashlight behind the bar.

She had just about given up hope when two Gremlins decided to grab her. Reacting instinctively, Kate picked up the nearest bottle and slammed one of them on the head. It collapsed onto the bar.

The other Gremlins reacted angrily and, hissing, rushed toward Kate. Realizing she had only a few moments, she lunged toward the cash register. That's when she saw the camera.

Dorry's Instamatic was carefully stashed behind the register. It had a flashcube, a perfect weapon that could open a pathway to freedom . . . if it worked.

Not allowing herself to dwell on this, Kate turned, pointed the camera at the swarming Gremlins, and pushed the button.

Psheee—ick!

A sudden burst of light from the flashbulb created an immediate path at the bar as Gremlins tumbled backward and over each other in their reaction to the pain. Kate raced five feet toward the doorway before the monsters recovered. A second click allowed her to plow six feet ahead. Now the front door was only ten feet away. Kate pushed the button again.

Nothing happened.

The Gremlins swarmed all over her, pushing her to the floor. Kate could feel pinpricks of pain all through her body as they tore at her. But even as she fell, she saw a huge flash of light against the front wall. The giggles of vengeful glee turned to howls of pain as the Gremlins scattered to the shadows.

The light was coming from a car outside, and it poured into the building. Kate scrambled to her feet, and raced for the door. A moment later, she felt the cold welcome air against her face.

A familiar voice called her name. It was Billy!

"Kate!" he shouted. "Get in."

Even as he spoke, however, the weakly idling car shuddered and died.

Billy tried to start the engine again as Kate hopped inside. The Gremlins, meanwhile, furious at having lost their prey, began heaving bottles and heavy ashtrays at the car.

"Let's run for it," Billy said, grabbing the knapsack with Gizmo inside.

A few minutes later, Billy and Kate found themselves drawn toward the safety of the bank. They raced inside the building and turned on the overhead lights. But the light caused Kate to gasp. Everything in the bank had been destroyed. Furniture lay on its side, and torn money was everywhere.

Hearing a soft moan, Kate and Billy followed the sound into the back vault. Inside sat Gerald Hopkins. He was staring straight ahead, as if hypnotized. On the floor next to him lay Mr. Corben.

"Gerald," Billy said. "Are you all right?"

Hopkins replied in a singsong voice. "You're too tall to be in this bank. This is the first bank just for little green people. And I'm the president."

Billy and Kate looked at each other.

"If you ask me, his buttons are in the wrong buttonholes," Kate said. "He's as soft as a week-old cantaloupe."

Gerald just stared straight ahead.

Billy and Kate heard a sudden noise outside the building. Moving to a side window, they saw hundreds of Gremlins marching down the street, their clawed feet scraping metallically against the concrete. Fascinated, Kate and Billy watched as the creatures entered the Colony movie theatre at the end of the block.

"Looks like the show must be starting," Kate said with a grin.

Billy glanced at his watch. It was almost four o'clock.

"It's not long until dawn," he said. "They must be heading for the theatre because there are no windows. That way they won't have to face the light."

"Maybe we should tell the police," Kate suggested.

"I tried that already," Billy said. "And where are they? Maybe I'd better handle this while there's still time."

Billy and Kate trotted across the street.

By the time they arrived at the theatre, it was packed with Gremlins. They sat in the seats just like unruly youngsters—talking, fighting, throwing popcorn at one another. Standing in the back of the lobby, hidden from the Gremlins' view, Billy smiled.

"It's perfect," he said. "Every last one of them must be here. It's the chance of a lifetime."

"For what?" Kate asked.

"To blow them up before they escape."

"Blow them up? How?" Kate asked.

"I used to work in this theatre after school," Billy said. "If it still has the same boiler problems, we may be in business."

"I don't get it."

"The boiler used to build up pressure, but instead of having it replaced, the owner put on a cheap valve to hold the pressure down. If I can close that valve, we can blow up the whole theatre."

"Yeah—and maybe us with it," she muttered.

"That's possible. Maybe you'd better leave now."

Kate shrugged. "You might need help," she said.

After waiting until the coast was clear, Billy and Kate crept down the steps to the basement and began their search for the valve in the darkness.

"I found it!" Billy shouted. "And the pressure's already really high."

He grabbed a wrench from the top of the boiler and turned the valve until it was closed.

"Now let's get out of here," he said.

They stumbled through the musty basement until they located a small iron door at the rear and pushed their way out.

"This way," Billy shouted, heading across the street.

They were halfway down the block when Kate shouted, "Suppose it doesn't—"

Her question was interrupted by a crash and a grinding noise so loud it seemed as if all the machinery in the world were breaking down at once. They ran for cover behind a parked car. A split second later, a huge flash of flame rose from the basement all the way up to the roof. Three blasts followed in quick succession, forcing the theatre's sides outward, like an oil tanker being torpedoed. In a minute the whole building was on fire.

"It worked," Billy said.

Kate, smiling at his understatement, could only nod.

Their crouching position behind the car was perfect for watching all three exits. Through the holes in the theatre wall they could see the forms of the dying Gremlins.

Another minute passed. The roar, so loud at first,

gradually diminished to a steady hiss. All sign of movement inside the movie house disappeared.

"I think we got all of them," Billy said finally.

The words were hardly out of his mouth, however, when they spotted a lone Gremlin. It stumbled through the charred front door of the crumbling structure and paused for a moment as if in a state of shock. Then it shook its distinctive, white-maned head and started across the street.

"Stripe!" Billy heard himself shout. "NO, NO, NO!"

CHAPTER SIX

It was well after four o'clock in the morning. The snow on the roads had turned to ice. Driving was perilous, but Mr. Peltzer kept his foot hard on the accelerator as he drove toward Kingston Falls.

He was terrified. He had been at a sales meeting in Middletown all day. Afterward he had heard nothing but TV and radio reports concerning the mysterious events at home. Most of the town's telephones were out, apparently sabotaged by the "green demons," so there had been no way of finding out if his wife and son were safe. Rather than spend the night worrying, he had decided to get in the car and risk the icy roads.

The journey seemed endless, partly because there were so many detours. As he moved along, the radio issued a string of bulletins from Kingston Falls, each describing some new calamity. Mr. Futterman . . . Mrs. Deagle . . . Stores and offices he had visited only days before were torn to pieces by unknown forces. What was going on, anyway?

It was nearly dawn when he pulled off Highway 46 onto Main Street. Just ahead he could see an orange glow and billows of smoke. The sight was made even stranger because there were no fire engines and no spectators. It was incredible. A major fire in Kingston Falls without a crowd? Impossible. Yet there it was, before his own eyes.

"Let my family be all right," he prayed.

The fire, he noted, was coming from the Colony Theatre, or what was left of it. Except for the flames, there was no movement. And then—

Crossing the street directly in his path appeared a—a what? Hitting the brakes hard, Mr. Peltzer brought the car to a complete stop. There was barely time to see the strange thing moving away in the dim light. Mr. Peltzer saw only a dark green back with horny plating, like something out of the dinosaur age. The creature—or person wearing a costume—disappeared into the department store by an open side door.

"What the heck's going on here?" Mr. Peltzer said aloud. "What *was* that thing?"

A few seconds later, his mouth fell open as he spotted two more figures. One of them was his son!

Leaping out of the car, he grabbed Billy in a bear hug. "You're O.K., son," he said. "Is your mom all right?"

"I guess she's O.K.," Billy said. "I'll tell you everything later. Now we've got to catch that Gremlin."

"That what?"

"Gremlin. They were all over town, but this is the last one."

"I saw something weird go in that door," Mr. Peltzer said, pointing toward the department store.

"Good."

With that, Billy grabbed Kate's hand and ran toward the building. His father followed.

"Wait a minute," Mr. Peltzer wheezed. "These guys are dangerous. You'd better let the cops handle it."

"They lost their chance," Billy yelled over his shoulder.

A few seconds later, he, Kate, and Gizmo disappeared into the store.

For a moment, Mr. Peltzer stood, puzzled. Then he too went into the store. "I may be old and out of shape," he said, "but maybe I can do something."

Inside the huge store, Billy peered through the dim light.

"Stripe couldn't have picked a better place to hide," he whispered.

The interior showrooms seemed to stretch completely out of sight. In fact, the store covered four acres. The aisles, which seemed longer than football fields, were jammed with displays. The only light came from small amber bulbs at the intersections of the aisles.

"He could hide in here forever," Billy said. "Unless we can flush him out by turning on the overheads."

Kate nodded. "I've been in this store a lot," she said. "There's a control panel in a room just off the main office. All the lights and stuff are activated from there. If we can get into that room, we should be able to flood the place."

"Good," Billy said. "Why don't you take Gizmo? I'll keep looking for Stripe in the meantime."

Kate started off, knapsack in hand. Gizmo streched out his paw as he saw Billy recede into the darkness.

"Sorry, little fella," Billy called. "It'll be easier if I take this trip alone."

Looking at Gizmo for a moment, Billy couldn't believe how many bad things had happened because of this one cute little creature. He allowed himself only this one moment for reflection, though, before he sprang back into action.

Billy grabbed a baseball bat from a nearby rack and started down the long aisle. He didn't even try to pretend he wasn't afraid. Every department he passed had items that could be used to wipe him out. In the sports department, he could be shot at by a rifle, struck with weights, hit with a tennis racket, or strangled with a jump rope. In the automotive section, there were tire wrenches, snow chains, hubcaps. In the Lawn Care Center, he could be struck with a rake or a shovel.

"Stop imagining things," he whispered to himself. "You're letting yourself get carried away."

The words were hardly out of his mouth when a bright silver object passed in front of his eyes and tore into the wall behind him, grazing Billy's cheek as it whizzed by. He spun around, sensing the approach of a second object.

Hurling himself to the floor, he felt it zoom directly over his head.

Thwack!

Rolling behind a cardboard display box, he lay on his stomach. From that position, he watched the second silver object hit the wall beside the first. The objects were rotary saw blades with sharp metal teeth.

The familiar giggle that followed left no doubt as to who had thrown them. Before Billy could get to his feet, Stripe leaped from behind a counter, unleashing a steady barrage of the blades. The missiles quickly shredded the display box Billy tried to use for protection.

When the saw blades were all used up, Stripe threw hammers, wrenches, small cans of paint, just about everything he could get a grip on with his claws. He eventually ran out of ammunition, however, muttering in Mogwai when he hurled the last object. Then he spun away and ran down another aisle.

Billy waited a moment before following, doubly wary now of a new ambush. "Darn it," he gasped as he ran. "I could use some light in this place."

* * *

Gizmo shivered in the store's control room when he heard the noise halfway across the building. It sounded as if a wall were collapsing. The heavy silence that followed was even worse, though. Gizmo imagined Billy trapped in a pile of wreckage or bleeding to death from a wound inflicted by Stripe. Frustrated, Gizmo decided he could no longer sit and wait. He had to help somehow. He flipped down the knapsack cover, climbed out of the bag, and lowered himself to the floor.

Once out of the control room, he wasn't sure where to go. He hated his short legs, which had not been created for speed. A moment later, however, he came upon something he knew would help.

It was a model sports car. Nearly two feet long and pink with red stripes, it was a battery-operated replica of a Corvette Stingray. Gizmo knew immediately it was just the thing to help speed him on his way. Hopping into the driver's seat, he flipped the switch to ON. He was nearly thrown out by the car's sudden movement forward, but he quickly regained his balance. He grabbed the steering wheel and was soon moving confidently down the long aisleway.

* * *

Half the length of the store away, Stripe could barely suppress a giggle of satisfaction. He was about to catch Billy in a very neat trap. That trap was nothing more than a long narrow room with only one way in and out. There were no nooks and crannies to hide in, no cartons or boxes to use for cover, no closets to duck into.

The room was the Electronics Center. It consisted of a vast display area for stereo equipment and TV sets, all neatly mounted in the walls. Once Billy entered he would be a sitting duck for Stripe's arrows.

Stripe had picked up a bow and a dozen steel-tipped arrows as he passed the far end of the sports department. Now he lay in wait for Billy to walk into his trap.

Unaware of Stripe's whereabouts, Billy was headed to the very end of the alcove. Stripe slid out of his hiding place and got the first arrow ready. He aimed the bow at an imaginary X between the young man's shoulder blades.

* * *

Meanwhile, in the store's control room, Kate was nearly in tears. Punching buttons at random, she had succeeded in turning on the Christmas decorations at the south end of the store, but so far she had had no luck with the overheads.

"Come on," she said. "Give me the overheads."

But there was no way of knowing. All she could do was continue pushing buttons, hoping she hit the right one.

* * *

Stripe pulled the bowstring as tight as he could make it and checked again to make sure Billy was in his line of sight.

"Attention, please!" a loud voice suddenly boomed.

Shocked, Stripe lost control of the arrow, which flew from the bow, striking a TV screen a foot above Billy's head.

"Attention, please," the announcer continued. "The store will close in ten minutes. Please complete any last-minute shopping so that our employees will be able to enjoy the rest of the evening."

Stripe cursed in Mogwai, wondering how the announcement had started just at the moment he was ready to send off his first arrow. The recorded announcement, of course, had been activated by Kate.

Stripe shrugged, picked up a second arrow, and sent it flying at the dodging Billy. It tore through his jacket at the neckline.

"Darn," Billy muttered. "For a Gremlin, he's a good shot!"

Looking around for a possible escape route, he

found nothing. All he could do was continue dodging until help came, Kate found the overhead lights, or Stripe ran out of arrows. Charging the Gremlin was probably suicidal, since it would make him a bigger and easier target to hit.

A third arrow headed his way, faster and more accurate than the others. Billy hit the floor, feeling it shoot by his ear.

Angry at having missed three times and determined to finish off his prey, Stripe readied another arrow. This time he aimed it not at Billy's head but at his chest. Now there would be no chance of missing. Pulling the string taut, he checked his aim again and prepared to send the arrow on its way.

At that moment, the overhead lights in the Electronics Center went on.

Stripe shrieked and dropped the bow and arrow. Scrambling toward a nearby aisleway that was still dark, he quickly disappeared around the corner.

As he started after Stripe, Billy heard his father's voice behind him, yelling something about waiting for the police. He knew it made sense, but it was more important to get Stripe now. Racing into the darkness toward Stripe's retreating form, he breathed a prayer that something else would not interfere with his capturing the last Gremlin.

* * *

From the store's control room, Kate had seen the lights go on in the Electronics Center.

"Lucky but dumb," she said. "Well, maybe this will turn on the rest."

She jabbed at some buttons on the panel.

A recorded voice began to speak. "Ladies and gentlemen," it said. "We now direct your attention to the northernmost end of the store, where our beautiful fountain is being turned on for the day. This fountain is so beautiful it is already known throughout the state. We hope you enjoy it."

* * *

As he ran down the aisle, Billy heard the announcement. The significance of it did not occur to him until he heard the gentle burbling in the distance. Then, playing the announcement back in his mind, he almost broke into tears.

"Fountain!" he shouted. "That means water . . . No! No!"

He continued to run toward the greenhouse at the far end of the store, but now there was despair in his expression rather than hope. Stripe was already there and had seen the fountain with its inviting water. From twenty feet above the floor, sheets of water tumbled down through rainbow-colored rock sculptures to a large pool at the bottom.

Seeing Billy race toward him, Stripe giggled triumphantly. Then he slowly tilted his body backward into the flowing water. . . .

The sight turned Billy's legs to strands of limp spaghetti. Leaning against the entrance wall, he slid to the floor, thinking only of the four times he had failed to capture Stripe—at home . . . at the YMCA . . . at the theatre . . . and now here. Each was a painful reminder of how things could go wrong.

Already he could hear the faint popping sound as the bubbles that would become new Gremlins began to erupt on Stripe's skin.

* * *

Gizmo, still at the wheel of the miniature Stingray, rolled through the entrance of the greenhouse and saw the worst in a glance. There was Billy, leaning against the wall, a picture of despair. Stripe was in the fountain. Nothing could be done to prevent more Gremlins from hatching and attacking the whole world.

Unless . . .

His gaze moved quickly from floor to ceiling. Gizmo saw a ray of hope. The huge tarpaulin covering the glass ceiling gave him an idea. Nearly crashing into the wall as he headed for the hanging rope that controlled the tarpaulin, Gizmo grabbed and released the rope in one quick, desperate motion. He then fell to the floor, first striking the hood of the car.

Lying flat on his back, he saw the rope fly toward the ceiling. The canvas tarpaulin rolled away from the glass ceiling. The long narrow strips parted, allowing a flood of early-morning sunlight into the large room. A bluish white path cut its way across the greenhouse, falling directly on Stripe in the fountain. Magnified and focused by the glass, the light pouring through the ceiling fell on Stripe like a laser beam. He screamed in pain but was unable to move. The heat attacked the bubbles forming on his skin, causing them and Stripe to blister, smolder, and die.

A gray mist rose slowly from the fountain as the last act in the night's terrible drama came to an end.

EPILOGUE

It was the day after Christmas, and Kingston Falls was still talking about the Gremlin invasion. Billy, sitting at home with Kate, Gizmo, and his parents, wanted only to forget about it and begin leading a normal life again. He smiled, recalling that just a few days before he had been unhappy because his life was so boring.

It was evening, and the family had just finished watching the news. Suddenly the doorbell rang.

"I hope it's not another reporter," Mrs. Peltzer said.

She went to the door. There standing before her was an elderly Oriental man, the wind blowing through his scraggly white hair. His expression was angry but controlled, the look of a parent who must punish his child.

Although Billy had never seen the man, he knew immediately who he was. And why he had come.

"I'm here for the Mogwai," the Chinese man said.

He looked past Mrs. Peltzer, catching sight of her husband.

As Mrs. Peltzer indicated he should enter, Gizmo suddenly became aware of the Chinese man's voice. Chirping excitedly, he bounded toward his old friend, covering the distance in four great leaps. Lifting the Mogwai and nuzzling it gently, the Chinese man smiled.

"I've missed you, my friend," he said.

Billy was touched and saddened. He could see that Gizmo and the man understood and loved each other.

"Now just a minute," Mr. Peltzer said, moving toward the Chinese man. "That little fella belongs to my son. I paid good money for him."

"I did not accept the money," the man said. "My grandson did that, and he has been punished as a result."

He reached into his coat and pulled out some bills, which he handed to Mr. Peltzer.

Billy's father frowned. "It's not that simple," he said. "It's not just money anymore."

"It's all right, Dad," Billy said. "I understand."

"I warned you," the Chinese man said to Mr. Peltzer. "With Mogwai comes much responsibility. But you didn't listen."

Gizmo, nestled comfortably in the old man's arms, felt a surge of sadness. If only he could tell Billy how he felt, or at least say something! Closing his eyes, he concentrated deeply. Then his mouth opened and human words came forth, the first he had ever said.

"Bye, Billy," he said.

"He talked!" Billy cried, happy and sad at the same time.

"You have accomplished a great deal," the Chinese man said. "We will always remember you."

He nodded and turned.

"Good evening," he said.

As they went out into the cold night, Gizmo lifted his furry paw in a little wave. Billy waved back, then shut the door quickly. He did not want to watch as they moved slowly into the darkness and out of his life.

MY FAVOURITE BOOK OF WITCHES AND
WIZARDS by Gillian Osband; illustrated by Caroline
Macdonald Paul

Did you know that a witch could change herself
into a hare at night by saying this spell ?

I shall goe into an hare
With sorrow and such and much care,
I shall goe in the devil's name,
Until I come home again.

Enchanting stories; facts and legends; extraordinary
spells; poems and a Witch's A-Z make this a fascinating
book.

0 552 52249X   £1.50

THE FOX AT DRUMMERS' DARKNESS
by Joyce Stranger

At Drummers' Darkness, in the dead of night, a triumphant army marched to battle. Just before dawn, the ghostly army returned; slow, dead and sorrowful — terrifying the moor.

The red fox was safe at Drummers' Darkness. Men never went there !

But that long, hot summer the haunting drumbeats became louder and louder — warning of danger. And the fox, in his desperate effort to find food, played a vital part in saving the town from disaster.

0 552 52159 0   85p

SPOOKY STORIES 5 edited by Barbara Ireson

Bogg the Body Snatcher who practised his evil trade on fresh young victims long after his remains had mouldered in the grave . . .

The Pharoah Hound who rose from a mummified corpse to defend the treasures of a long-dead boy king . . .

A phantom child who cried for a companion to join him in his eternal play . . .

These special creatures appear in a delicious brew of supernatural tales, written by such masters as Philippa Pearce, Joan Aiken, and Agatha Christie to chill the blood as it courses through your unsuspecting veins . . .

0 552 52230 9   95p